THE VAMPIRE RULES

DARK WORLD: THE VAMPIRE WISH PREQUEL NOVELLA

MICHELLE MADOW

DREAMSCAPE PUBLISHING

JACEN

"To the gold!" my teammate Ryan said, raising a shot of vodka in the air.

"To the gold!" I repeated.

We clinked our glasses together, tapped the bottoms on the table, and drank.

"We couldn't have done it without you." Zane looked at me, giving me a slight nod of appreciation.

"Hell yeah!" Ryan reached for his shot glass and started banging it rhythmically on the table. "Jacen. Jacen. Jacen," he chanted, the other guys quickly joining along.

I smiled modestly, although I knew they were right. Without my four second win on the final relay of the event, we would have lost the gold that had secured us the all-around win.

This was a major step in what I'd been training for all my life—the Olympics.

"What's up?" Ryan asked me once everyone had finished chanting. "You got all serious all of a sudden."

"Just thinking about a year and a half from now." I leaned back and smirked, not wanting to look *too* serious.

"Now's not the time to think about the Olympics." He raised his empty shot glass. "Now's the time to celebrate the win we had *today*!"

"Why's the 'next Phelps' worrying about the Olympics?" Zane asked. "Everyone knows you're a shoe in."

"No one's a shoe in," I said. "Who knows what could happen between now and then?"

"I'll tell you what could happen between now and then." Ryan belched, rested his elbows on the table, and looked toward the bar. "See that hottie all alone at the end of the bar?"

I looked in the general direction. With her long dark hair, porcelain skin, and doll-like features, the girl was impossible to miss.

Her eyes met mine, and I quickly turned away, not wanting to be caught staring.

"Hot, right?" Ryan asked.

"For sure," I said, even though she was more than hot—she was gorgeous.

"She's been checking you out all night."

"Has she?" I raised an eyebrow—intrigued, but not surprised. As a group of champion swimmers, my teammates and I weren't good at blending in. But while I enjoyed an occasional fling, I never allowed anything to get further than that. I didn't need anyone—especially a girl—distracting me from my Olympic dream.

"Twenty bucks says you can get her up to your room in twenty minutes or less," Zane said, slapping a twenty on the table.

"It's gonna take longer than that." Ryan put a twenty down as well. "She's way too uppity. Not dressed like a typical groupie."

I sneaked another glance at her—Ryan was right. I didn't know much about women's clothes, but hers looked expensive. Plus, she was barely showing any cleavage.

It was a scientific fact that the lower the cut of a woman's top, the easier it was to get her into bed.

Well, maybe not *completely* scientific. But my teammates and I had put the theory to the test a few months ago, and it generally proved true.

She said something to the bartender and smiled. It

was a knowing sort of smile—as if she was in on a secret that the rest of the world wasn't a part of. She also only had water in front of her, which made me wonder if she was of legal drinking age.

If she weren't, she would have been asked to leave the bar, right?

Usually that was the case. But from the mesmerized way the bartender stared at her, he looked like he would risk getting into trouble for the chance to talk to her all night.

"Yo, Olympian!" Zane snapped his fingers in front of my face.

He was looking at me like he was waiting for me to answer a question.

"Yeah?" I said.

"What do you say?" he asked. "You up for the challenge?"

I glanced over at the girl again—subtly, of course—and our eyes quickly met.

My teammates were right. She was definitely checking me out.

The guys and I had come down to the hotel bar to celebrate our win. We had an early flight home tomorrow morning, so I hadn't intended on making this a big night out. After all, I'd be jumping back into training tomorrow.

But there was something about the girl that made me want to talk to her. Plus, the guys knew me well.

I never turned down a challenge.

So I stood up and headed toward the bar.

2

JACEN

I MADE a ruse of surveying the open spaces at the bar, as if figuring out where there was room for me to go in to grab a drink. Eventually, I honed in on the empty barstool next to the girl.

Normally the seats next to the most beautiful women filled up the quickest. But hey, I wasn't complaining.

I slid into the space next to her, although I didn't sit down. I didn't pay attention to her at all. Instead, I focused on the bartender.

Once I caught his eye, I flashed him my credit card —the universal symbol for "I'm ready to place my order."

He nodded in acknowledgment as he whipped up complicated cocktails for two older women on the other side of the bar.

I put my credit card away—I wouldn't need it, since I was staying at the hotel.

As I waited, I rested an elbow on the bar, glancing at the girl out of the corner of my eye. She was even more beautiful up close. Dare I say flawless. I was stunned for a second, but quickly got a hold of myself.

"Only a water?" I asked, glancing at her drink.

For a pick up line, it wasn't much. But I rarely had to try hard. All that mattered was getting an in.

"For now." She spoke with a lilting accent, giving me the same knowing smile she'd used on the bartender earlier.

"Where are you from?" I asked.

"Guess." She tilted her head, her hair falling gently down her shoulders and alongside her breasts. I wasn't sure if she'd done it on purpose or not, but it definitely got me looking.

"I'll need to hear you say more than that if you expect me to guess," I said.

"Like what?" She leaned forward, looking intrigued.

"How about you tell me your name," I started. "And your drink of choice, so I can buy one for you. You *are* legal drinking age, right?"

"You have no idea." She laughed, her eyes lighting up in amusement.

"What's that supposed to mean?"

"Nothing," she said, serious again. "I'm nineteen, so yes, that's legal drinking age here in Toronto. And my favorite drink is red wine. Amarone, to be precise."

"Interesting." Most of the girls I picked up at bars chose fruity drinks, with a beer thrown in here and there. "And your name?" I asked.

"Laila," she answered. "I take it you're Jacen?"

"How did you know?" I assumed Ryan was wrong and she *was* a swimming groupie, but she looked classier than that. Those girls also normally traveled in packs.

"Your friends over there were chanting it earlier." She glanced at the table full of my teammates.

They looked away the moment she turned to them, doing a terrible job of pretending that they weren't watching us like we were their entertainment for tonight.

"Right," I said sheepishly, remembering how they'd chanted like a bunch of frat boys. "We won the gold today in a major competition."

"I heard there was some big event nearby," she said. "What sport do you play?"

I smiled, relieved that she *wasn't* a groupie who'd come to our hotel to pick one of us up for the night. "Swimming," I said.

"Nice." She ran her eyes down my body, checking me out.

From the way the small smile remained on her lips, I assumed she liked what she saw.

"You said your team won," she continued. "But from the way your friends were chanting, it sounded like *you* won the gold."

"I won a few individual races." I smirked and leaned closer to her. She smelled delicious—like a sweet, intoxicating flower.

Her gaze locked on mine, her eyes a stunning shade of blue that reminded me of the Pacific Ocean. Despite her proper demeanor, she leaned closer and licked her lips, as if daring me to kiss her.

"So." The bartender smacked his hands down on the surface in front of us, pulling me out of the moment. "What'll it be?"

I got ahold of myself, remembering that I'd come over here under the guise of grabbing a drink. "The best IPA you have on tap for me," I said. "And an Amarone for the lady."

"Got it." He didn't ID Laila, so I assumed he must have covered that when she'd sat down.

I told him my room number so he could put it on my bill.

"Want to keep the tab open?" he asked.

I glanced at Laila.

She simply raised an eyebrow, as if curious about my answer herself.

"Sure." I slid into the seat next to her, like I was only *now* deciding to join her. "Let's keep it open."

He walked away to get our drinks, and I returned my focus to Laila, glad she looked pleased by my decision to stay.

"So." She crossed one leg over the other, her foot nearly brushing mine. "Have you figured out where I'm from?"

She'd entranced me so much that I hadn't given my original question another thought. But now that she mentioned it, I wracked my mind for a possible answer. Her accent sounded like she came from a place where English was the official language, but I couldn't pinpoint the country.

"South Africa?" I guessed, since that was an English speaking country where I was less familiar with the accent.

"Nope."

"Australia?"

"Wrong again."

"England?"

"Finally." She smiled. "I thought you'd never get it."

"Your accent sounds different from other British ones I've heard," I told her. "It threw me off my game."

"I'm one of the few remaining people on Earth who still speaks this dialect." She had that mysterious look in her eyes again, like she was sharing a coveted secret.

I was about to ask her more, but the bartender returned and placed our drinks in front of us before I had the chance.

I picked up my glass and raised it in a toast. "To new friends," I said, holding my gaze with hers.

"And to unexpected evenings," she added. "In the absolute best of ways."

She clinked her glass with mine, and we drank.

3

JACEN

"So, what are you doing here in Toronto?" I asked, settling into my place next to her at the bar.

"Family trip," she said simply.

"You're here with your family, yet at a hotel bar by yourself?"

"My family goes to sleep early," she explained. "But I've always been more of the nocturnal type."

"A night owl?" I asked.

"A vampire." She chuckled and sipped her wine, eyeing up my reaction.

It was a bit of a strange comment, but someone as stunning as Laila could get away with saying anything. "You're into all that fantasy stuff?" I guessed.

"You could say that." She smiled—she looked so mysterious when she smiled. "I do enjoy reading."

"So do I," I said. "I don't get to do much of it anymore, since I'm always training, but I read a lot when I was younger."

We continued chatting from there—Laila proved to be an excellent conversationalist. It wasn't long before both of our drinks were empty. I'd met my fair share of girls on the road, but never ones as intelligent, sophisticated, and as beautiful as Laila. I could talk to her all night.

"Your friends keep looking over at us." She glanced over my shoulder at where my teammates were sitting.

A quick glance at my watch showed me that Laila and I had been chatting for longer than twenty minutes. Ryan would be thrilled that he won the bet. But I didn't look back at the guys. They'd likely had a few more drinks by now, and the last thing I needed was for them to do something to embarrass me.

"Want to check out another place?" I asked. "There are some other bars on this street where we can continue this conversation *without* having my drunk teammates as an audience."

She set her empty wine glass down and tilted her head, once more looking like she was up to something.

Who *was* this girl, and how had I fallen under her spell so easily?

"You should invite me to your room." Her voice

sounded like music, and my entire body relaxed—that IPA must have been stronger than I'd realized. "There are a few desserts on the room service menu that I've had my eye on since checking in. And we *certainly* won't have to worry about an audience there."

I smiled lazily, since I could gladly grant her request.

"Would you like to come up to my room?" I stood and held an arm out to her, not bothering to glance in my teammates' direction. All that mattered right now was Laila. "You can order anything off the room service menu that you want."

"That sounds divine." She stood and looped her arm in mine, gazing up at me with those hypnotizing blue eyes. "Please, lead the way."

And so, I did.

4

JACEN

I OPENED the bottle of wine that the hotel had left in my room when I'd checked in, and then called down to room service.

"I'd like one of each of your desserts," I ordered.

Laila had just opened the menu, but she closed it after I'd spoken. Her lips curved up, and she tossed her hair over her shoulder, apparently impressed.

Once my order was confirmed, I placed the phone back down and poured us each a glass of wine. She walked up to join me and took her glass.

"That was very thoughtful of you," she said, lifting her glass in a toast. "You're quite the gentleman. I have less work cut out for me than I'd anticipated."

"What do you mean?" I immediately jumped to

where most girls tended to go—that she saw this escalating into a relationship. And while she was entrancing, I refused to let *anything* distract me from my training. "My plane leaves in the morning, and with you living in England and me in the States, I don't want to give you the wrong idea..."

"I understand." She lifted her chin and raised her glass higher. "To tonight?"

"To tonight." I clinked her glass, since *that* was certainly a toast I could get behind.

I took a sip of the wine—a full red that had a slight sweetness to it. It was perfect for dessert.

She smiled after tasting hers, and I was glad that the hotel had chosen well. The moonlight shined through the windows, making her porcelain skin look like it was glowing, and I wanted so badly to kiss her.

But I didn't want to rush this. After all, room service would be coming soon.

I wanted to save the best part of the night for *after* dessert.

"What?" She smiled up at me, laughing nervously.

I was surprised. Up until now, I didn't think a girl as confident and sophisticated as Laila was capable of being nervous. Hell, *I* normally didn't get nervous, but being around her made me dizzier than ever. Everything about her entranced me—her voice, her eyes, her scent, her smile. It was like she was putting a spell on me.

"You're beautiful," I said honestly. "I'm glad we met tonight."

"I'm glad we met, too," she said. "Despite your teammates having to put you up to it."

"You heard that?" I stilled, embarrassed.

"Oh, Jacen." She sighed, as if I were a clueless child. "I know far more than you could ever imagine."

Another cryptic statement.

I was about to ask what she meant, but there was a knock on the door.

"Room service," the person called from the other side.

I opened the door, and the server rolled in a cart topped with every dessert on the menu. I gave him a nice tip, and after setting up our table, he was on his way.

"What'll it be?" I asked Laila, motioning to the display before us.

"I don't know." She smiled coyly and twisted a strand of hair around her finger. "What do *you* want?"

"Ladies first," I said, since two could play *this* game. "I insist."

She chose the molten lava cake. I wasn't surprised, since girls usually went for chocolate. But I rarely ate dessert—I had to stay in shape for training—so I went for the fruit bowl.

"You're not going to indulge?" Laila raised an eyebrow. "You're missing out." She savored a bite of her cake, looking extraordinarily sexual while doing so.

With her gazing at me like that, how could I refuse?

I replaced my fruit bowl with the apple pie a la mode and took a bite. She was right—the dessert *was* delicious.

"That's more like it," she said, taking another bite of her cake.

We tried everything on the platter until we were so full that we might burst. Once finished, there was still a decent amount left over. But given the amount we'd started with, we did a pretty good job.

"What was your favorite?" I asked, finally laying my spoon down in defeat.

"I haven't tasted my favorite yet." She slithered over to me and sat on my lap, draping an arm around my neck.

"Oh yeah?" I was surprised by her boldness, but hey, I wasn't complaining. "What's your favorite?"

"You." She brought her lips to mine and quickly deepened the kiss, as if she'd been waiting for this moment all night.

I brushed my tongue against hers, enjoying the foreplay. She tasted as delicious as she smelled. Then I scooped her up and brought her to the bed, laying her down and hovering above her. She gazed up at me with those big blue eyes, and I smiled at the knowledge that this beautiful creature was mine for the night.

I captured her mouth in mine again and lowered my body on top of hers, not wanting any space left between us.

She arched up to meet me, and I reached for the bottom of her top, starting to remove it. I couldn't wait to see her body—I bet it was as beautiful and as perfect as the rest of her.

But her hand rushed to mine, stopping me.

"What?" I was confused—I thought she wanted this.

She flipped me over with more strength than I'd given her credit for, and she straddled me, smirking down at me. "Not yet, Jacen." Her voice sounded different than before—sharper and crueler. "There'll be time for all of that—and more—later. But first, I need to taste you."

Before I could ask what she meant, she smiled—revealing sharp fangs that *definitely* hadn't been there earlier—lowered her head to my neck, and pierced my skin.

I tried to push her off of me, but she gripped my wrists and pinned them above my head. I struggled, but it was no use—my strength was nothing compared to hers.

How was that *possible*? I was a future Olympian and she was a girl less than half my size.

She must have drugged me. She'd certainly had plenty of opportunities throughout the evening to slip something into my drink. It would also explain the fangs, because that *had* to be a hallucination.

"Crazy bitch!" I continued to struggle, even though it was futile. "Get *off* me!"

She lifted her head from my neck and smiled, my blood coating her lips. "Don't make another noise." Her voice took on that musical quality from when we'd been at the bar—when she'd asked me to invite her to her room.

I opened my mouth to scream again, but no sound came out. So I thrust my head forward and knocked it into hers, hoping to catch her unaware.

My head felt like it had collided with a brick wall. I fell back into the pillow, the world spinning around me.

Laila was unfazed.

"Stop fighting me." Her voice still had that musical quality, and as if by magic, I stopped struggling.

I *wanted* to fight, but I *couldn't*.

All I could do was stare up at her in terror.

"This will all be over soon," she said. "I promise." She

lowered her mouth to my neck again, and I felt colder and colder and she sucked the blood from my body.

I tried to stay awake, but eventually, there was no fighting it anymore.

The world grew hazy around the edges, and everything went dark.

5

JACEN

My throat was on fire, burning so badly that I couldn't swallow. It was the telltale sign of getting sick.

At least I'd picked up this virus *after* the Global Aquatics Championship. I'd have to take it easy with training the next few days, but I'd been able to help my team secure the gold. *That* was what mattered.

But it wasn't just my throat that didn't feel right. The rest of me felt empty, too. All the way down to my bones.

I was *starving*. I'd never been so hungry in my life.

How long had it been since I'd eaten?

I should get up, grab some medicine, and order breakfast. But the bed at the hotel was so comfortable. I wanted to go back to sleep until my alarm blared to wake me up for my flight.

But I couldn't get back to sleep. My mind was too busy racing with the crazy nightmare I'd had last night, of the beautiful woman who had come up to my room to drink my blood.

I hadn't had nightmares since I was a kid. But this one was burned into my mind so intensely that I doubted I would ever forget it.

Last night was pretty hazy, too. I must have had a few too many celebratory shots with the guys.

Maybe *that* was why I felt so awful.

I'd had my fair share of hangovers, but this one took the cake. Everything felt sensitive beyond belief. The footsteps from the hall were amplified so much that they pounded in my head, and a variety of smells assaulted my senses, so strong that I felt like I couldn't breathe.

To top it off, the burning in my throat kept getting worse and worse. I felt sicker than when I'd had the flu a few years ago.

I reached over to the nightstand to check the time, but my cell phone wasn't there. Weird. I always kept it next to me when I slept.

Reluctantly, I opened my eyes, threw off the blanket, and sat up.

She sat at the foot of the bed, still wearing the tight jeans and silky black top she'd had on last night.

Laila.

The girl from my nightmare.

And instead of being in the hotel, we were in a lavishly decorated, massive room that looked like it belonged in a palace.

I reached for the spot in my neck that she'd bitten last night, surprised that the skin was perfectly smooth —like it had never been bitten at all.

Whatever drug she'd given me must have made me hallucinate the entire biting scenario.

Hopefully that meant kissing her had been part of the hallucination, too.

"You," I growled, flexing my fists. "What the *hell* did you do to me?" I rushed forward to strangle her, but her hands wrapped around my wrists, and she pinned me to the bed just like she had last night.

Which apparently *hadn't* been a nightmare, and had actually happened.

"You're *much* stronger now than when you were human." She straddled her legs around my waist, pressing herself against me in a way that would have been sexy in any other situation. "But you won't reach your full potential until you feed. To this day, I still remember the pain following being turned. It makes a hangover seem pleasant, does it not?"

I had no idea what she was talking about.

But one thing was clear—the crazy bitch had drugged me and *abducted* me.

I needed to get out of here.

"If it's money you want, I have plenty of it," I said. "Let me go, and I'll send you whatever you want. I promise."

There was no way in hell I was giving her anything—other than reporting her to the cops and getting her arrested. But promising money was what heroes in action movies did all the time, so it was worth a try.

I'd promise her anything if it meant getting away from her and out of this place.

"Look around, Jacen." Her blue eyes no longer looked big and captivating. Now they were sharp and severe. "Does it look like I need your money?"

I took a deep breath, trying to remain calm despite every muscle in my body aching to fight. Because fighting wasn't getting me anywhere. Whatever drug she'd given me must have still been in my system, or I was coming down from it. That would explain why I felt like such shit.

Since I was in no condition to fight, I might as well try to talk her down from whatever she was trying to do to me.

"Is this your room?" I tried to sound as relaxed as I had when we'd chatted at the bar.

The more information I could get from her, the better.

"No," she said. "This is *your* room. Inside of *my* palace."

"*Your* palace?" I couldn't help but laugh at how absurd she sounded. "If you have an entire palace, then why did you need to abduct me?"

"I didn't abduct you," she said. "I *turned* you."

"What does that even *mean*?"

"It'll all make sense after you feed," she said. "Now, I'm going to let go for a second to call for your meal. I advise you not to fight me. Not only am I stronger than you in your weakened state, but there are guards stationed by the door. They won't be *nearly* as gentle with you as I've been." She pulled one of her hands away and ran a finger across my cheek, like she was studying me.

The feeling of her nail against my skin made me shudder in revulsion.

She must have mistaken my reaction for pleasure, because she smiled in triumph. "You'll be good and stay here, right, Jacen?" she asked.

"Of course." I held my gaze with hers, keeping all emotion from my voice. I couldn't let her hear how much she disgusted me. Not if I wanted a chance of getting out of here.

But *how* could I get out of here? I was strong, but there were armed guards outside the doors. I wasn't so delusional to think I stood a chance against guards with weapons.

All I could do was bide my time, assess the situation, and plan an escape.

So I did as she asked and made no attempt to run as she reached for her phone.

Her eyes stayed on me as she moved, her lips turning up in pleasure when I obeyed. I made sure to keep my gaze on hers. I might not be running, but that didn't mean I was weak.

"The new prince has awoken," she said to whoever was on the other line, sounding mighty pleased with herself as she spoke. "Bring his first meal up to his room now."

6

JACEN

"PRINCE?" I raised an eyebrow, pretty sure she'd been talking about me.

"It'll all be explained in time." She sat back down on the foot of my bed, still looking beyond pleased with herself. "But first you need to eat. Once you eat, you'll feel better. I promise."

"Unless the food contains the antidote to whatever drug you gave me, I doubt it'll make much difference." I narrowed my eyes, keeping my guard up despite the pain pounding in my head.

"I didn't drug you." She laughed, although her attention quickly turned to the door. "Do you hear that?" she asked, perking up. "Dinner's here."

She walked across a sitting room area and over to the doors to throw them open. A tall, buff man waited on the other side—I assumed he was one of the guards she was talking about. Next to him was a scrawny, older man in shackles.

She pulled a knife out of her boot and slashed it across the old man's neck.

The sweetest, most intoxicating scent I'd ever smelled filled the room, and my body exploded with pleasure. My gums ached with need, red filling my vision as I ran for what I desired—the blood pulsing out of the man's throat.

The next thing I knew, I was kneeling over his drained corpse. There wasn't even any more blood left from where it had landed on the hardwood floor. It looked like it had been licked clean.

Had *I* done that?

I stood and backed away in horror, my eyes locked on the man's empty gaze. His pupils were dilated so much that I could barely see the brown in his eyes. It was almost like he'd been drugged to death.

More horror set in as I realized I'd just drank his *blood*. That shouldn't have made me feel good.

Yet, the burning in my throat and the pounding in my head was starting to ease.

"The prince is still hungry," Laila purred from behind me.

"We'd prepared for this." The guard reached for his

phone and used it like a walkie-talkie to say, "Bring the next prisoner in."

The "next one" turned out to be a woman around my mom's age.

"Please," she begged, looking at me in terror. "Don't—"

She didn't have time to finish her sentence before the redness filled my vision again, and I pounced.

When I came to, she was crumpled on top of the old man's corpse.

Dead.

This continued until there were four human corpses in the pile.

In the middle of the fifth one—a male who looked around my age—I became aware of what I was doing. The redness cleared while my mouth was still attached to the twin holes in his neck. I heard myself moan as the most delicious liquid I'd ever tasted rolled down my throat, filling my body with a warm, Heavenly light.

The man went limp in my arms. If I didn't pull away soon, he would die.

But everything in me pulsed with need. My mind said, "stop," but my body said, "keep going."

My mind stood no chance against the fervent desire of my body. I didn't stop until I'd drained the man of his last drop of blood.

"No more." I dropped the body on the ground, studying it so I'd feel the full weight of the life I'd taken.

Once I'd memorized his face, I turned around and ran for Laila, wrapping my hands around her throat like she'd done to me earlier and forcing her to the floor.

"What have you *done* to me?" I yelled, bringing my face close to hers.

She just looked up at me and smiled, like she *enjoyed* being strangled.

Before I could scream at her to answer me—or to fight me, since I knew she could—the guards grabbed my arms and pulled me off of her. But I twisted out of their grasps and ran for the door. The pile of bodies before it was the only thing that made me pause.

The bodies of the people I'd *killed*.

In that split second pause, something pricked the back of my neck. An icy-hot pain burned through every vein in my body, all the way to the tips of my fingers and toes.

I screamed and fell down to my knees, shaking from the pain.

"That's better." Laila appeared between me and the doors, a needle of light green liquid in her hand. "I'd give you more to punish you for attacking me, but I suppose I can't blame your outburst, since I didn't exactly introduce myself properly the first time we met."

I just stared up at her, swallowed down the pain, and forced myself to stand. It hurt like Hell—like my joints were stiff and rusted from neglect—but I refused to remain on my knees in front of Laila like a pathetic, subdued weakling.

"Most would be writhing on the floor like a dying animal after the dose of wormwood I just gave you." Her eyes glinted as she watched me struggle to stand, like she was getting some kind of sick pleasure out of my pain. "But not my Jacen. You're strong. Just like I'd planned."

"What *are* you?" I asked, somehow forcing myself to speak through the pain.

"I already told you what I am—it was one of the first things I said to you. But of course, you didn't believe me." She stepped closer to me, sounding nothing like the sweet, flirty girl I'd met at the bar. "You thought I was joking. But maybe you'll take me more seriously now that you've had your first meal. Because I'm Laila, queen of the vampire kingdom of the Vale."

7

JACEN

I STARED at her in shock, unable to believe it. This was all insane. It had to be a nightmare.

But it *felt* real.

And the proof of what she'd said was right in front of me—the bodies I'd drained of blood. It was also in my memories, when she'd flashed her fangs and sank them into my neck back at my hotel room.

I should be dead, like those five humans I'd killed.

Yet I was here. Alive. I was stronger than ever, and I'd drank blood.

I didn't know much about vampires. I'd been too focused on my training to care about silly fantasy stories. But I knew enough to know that vampires turned people into vampires by biting them.

Was that what she'd meant when she'd said she'd *turned* me?

"You're silent, but I see you have many questions." Laila's gaze didn't leave my own. "After what I've put you through, you certainly deserve answers. So I'll give them to you... as long as you promise not to attack me again." She smiled sweetly, as if she was trying to flirt her way into getting me to agree.

We'd passed the stage where that would work a *long* time ago.

She might be beautiful, but when I looked at her now, all I saw was a monster. Especially when she pressed her thumb lightly enough on the syringe of the needle that a droplet of the torturous liquid—the *wormwood*—collected in a droplet on the tip. The poison was odorless, but the needle was still more than halfway full, which got the message across loud and clear.

Give her any more trouble, and I'd get a lot more than the dose she'd already shocked me with.

"Fine," I said, since despite my rage at her, I believed her when she said she was going to give me answers. I'd rather get them the easy way than the hard way. "I'll play nice—for now."

"Lovely." She capped the needle and secured it in her pocket. "My reflexes are faster than yours, so don't test me." She glanced over at the guards, who were watching her expectantly. "Leave," she commanded them. "And remove the trash on your way out."

She motioned toward the pile of corpses in front of the doors, making it clear what she'd meant by "the trash."

The guards did as she said, lifting the bodies with ease and taking them out of the room.

I couldn't believe that I'd killed all those people. Yet, the moment Laila had slit the first man's throat, the urge to drink his blood had been primal—so strong I couldn't resist it.

The worst part was that I'd *liked* it.

"So, where were we?" Laila asked with a smile.

"The part where you were telling me that you turned me into a monster." I held my gaze with her, my eyes cold.

"That's what you think I did?" she asked.

"I just killed five people in cold blood." I motioned to where their bodies had been on the floor. "So yes—that's what I *know* you did."

"About that," she said, clearing her throat. "You needed to drink from the vein to complete your transition. But until you learn to control your bloodlust, that feast was a one-time deal. So you'll be drinking bottled blood, like most of the vampires in the kingdom. Only once you gain control will you be granted the royal privilege to drink from the veins of the prisoners whenever you'd like."

"That won't be happening." I curled my hands into fists. "Because whatever you did to me, you're going to reverse it."

"That's impossible," she said. "The gift I've given you cannot be reversed."

"Gift?" I lifted a small vase from an end table and threw it across the room. It whizzed by Laila's head, missing her and shattering against the wall. "You turned me into a *monster!*"

She zipped toward me and jammed the needle into my arm.

Shattering pain wracked through my body. I yelled out in pain, crumpling to the floor. Darkness threatened my vision, but I blinked and took deep breaths, determined not to pass out.

Who knew what Laila would do to me if I did?

I eventually got ahold of myself enough to pull myself up onto the nearest sofa. It hurt too much to stand, but there was no way I was going to stay on the floor.

"Impressive." Laila raised an eyebrow and sat down on the sofa across from me. "That amount of wormwood would have knocked out most vampires. But you're strong. Just like I intended."

"That's the second time you've said that," I said. "You didn't turn me randomly, did you?"

"Of course not." She smiled. "I'd selected you long before stepping into the hotel bar where we met."

"Why?" Pain echoed in my voice, and I rested my elbows on top of my legs, feeling hopeless. "What did I do to deserve this?"

"You're strong," she said. "Disciplined. Motivated. Ambitious. By all reports, you were predicted to be the hero of the next Olympics. All of those traits—the traits of an Olympian athlete at the top of his or her game—they're the traits I was searching for. You see, the transition to become a vampire prince or princess is even much more challenging than the transition to become a regular vampire. Most don't survive it. So I searched and found you—the most talked about athlete for the next Olympic games. You survived the change, like I thought you would. And after what I've seen of you so far—the way you threw off those guards, your ability to withstand high doses of wormwood, and the exorbitant amount of blood you consumed for your first meal—choosing you was one of the best decisions I've ever made."

"But I don't want to be a monster," I said. "I'll kill myself before I lose control again and kill more people."

"No, you won't." She sounded so sure of herself—like

she knew me better than I knew myself. "I've turned many vampires who ended up doing such a thing, and they all handled their first kill with far less dignity than you managed today. You were born to be a vampire, Jacen. The sooner you accept it, the sooner you can enjoy the wealth, power, and most importantly—the *immortality*—that I gave you when I made you a prince of the Vale."

8

JACEN

I STARED HER DOWN, unwilling to accept it.

"People will know I'm missing," I said. "Like you said, I'm high profile. There are people searching for me right now, and they're going to find me. Just you wait."

"No one's coming for you," she said simply.

"What makes you so sure about that?" I asked.

"Because everyone thinks you're dead."

"What?" I narrowed my eyes at her, not willing to believe it. "Why would they think that?"

She reached for something—a remote control—and pressed a button to lower a gigantic flat screen television from the ceiling. "I recorded this just for you while you were going through the change," she said, turning the television on and clicking to a recorded news report on the DVR. "I thought you'd want to see it once you woke up."

The news report was already cued up—all Laila had to do was press play.

On the screen was the hotel I'd been staying at during the swim meet—with flames and smoke coming out of the top windows. The caption below the photo read, "Hotel bombing."

"We're here half past midnight reporting live at the Eastin Hotel in Toronto, where a terrorist has set off a bomb in one of the upper floors," a pretty newscaster said into a microphone. "It appears to have been a direct attack on the USA male swim team visiting the city for the Global Aquatics Championship, as the floor they were staying on was the one targeted. None of them have been located yet, and the rescuers on the scene say it doesn't look good. More coming on the hour."

Laila was emotionless as she fast-forwarded to the next update, where the newscaster announced that my teammates and I—along with many others staying at the hotel—were confirmed dead.

"Where are they?" I turned to Laila, fury in my eyes.

"Where are who?" she asked calmly.

"My teammates!" I said. "Are they in this place, too? Are you hedging your bets? Turning all of us into vampires and seeing who survives?"

"No," she said. "I already told you—I chose you specifically."

"So what did you do to my friends?" It took all of my self-control not to strangle her again. The only thing stopping me was the glint of the needle tucked away in her pocket. The pain from the first two doses of wormwood was still wrecking havoc through my system—I knew my body well enough to know I couldn't handle any more.

"They're dead," she said. "Blown up by the terrorist who bombed the hotel."

It took a few seconds for what she'd said to sink in.

Once it did, the weight of my teammates' deaths crushed me.

"You were the terrorist, weren't you?" I said. "You planted that bomb. You killed them all."

"Of course not." She laughed and pulled her hair over her shoulders. "As a vampire queen, I have the ability of compulsion. As a prince, you'll have compulsion too, once you learn how to harness it."

"What's compulsion?"

"Mind control," she said simply.

"You used it on me, didn't you?" I realized. "At the bar when you asked me to ask you up to your room, and after you'd bitten me, when you told me to stop talking and to stop fighting you."

"I did," she confirmed. "And I used it on a young Muslim man the night before I met you, when I gave him the supplies and instructions to carry out his task. He was a kind, peaceful man without a violent bone in his body, but men of his religion are easy scapegoats these days. ISIS was eager to take credit for the bombing despite having nothing to do with it at all."

"You're a monster." Disgust rolled through my body as I looked at her.

How many innocents had Laila killed in her immortal life? Did she have a heart at all?

"I'm a queen." She lifted her chin, holding her head high. "Queens make hard decisions for the sake of their kingdoms. If they don't, their kingdom will fall, and they'll reign no more. I'll do whatever it takes to make my kingdom the strongest it can be, and I'll always protect my subjects—especially the princes and princesses I sire. You'll see that in time."

"In the meantime," she continued. "You'll learn to control your bloodlust. Vampires need more blood when they're newly turned, so you'll be weaned down until you're drinking a normal amount each day. Then you'll be tested to ensure you're in control. As long as you're strong and disciplined—which I know you are, since that's why I chose you as my newest prince—you'll get through this and claim your rightful place in the Vale."

I could barely pay attention to what she was saying.

Because right now, my entire family thought I was *dead*. Blown into pieces.

But I *wasn't* dead. And as long as I was alive, there was a chance I could see my family again.

I would do anything to see them again—even if that meant playing nice with Laila so I could squeeze as much information out of her as possible.

Gathering information was a good goal. Because once I had enough information, I could figure out a plan to get out of here and go home. I didn't know what I would do with myself when I got home, but I could figure that out later.

Now, I needed to focus on escape.

"You're saying that I can learn to control this... bloodlust?" I watched Laila carefully as I spoke. "That I can stop myself from killing?"

"You *must* stop yourself from killing." She sat straighter, apparently happy with where this conversation was heading. "If a vampire can't maintain control of their bloodlust, they risk revealing our existence to humans. And while we're powerful and strong, humans outnumber us. The supernatural community as a whole is better off keeping humans in the dark—especially now that humans have created weapons that could obliterate us with the touch of a button."

"And what about the vampires who can't control their bloodlust?" I asked.

"Like I told you before, I chose you because of your determination, discipline, strength, and ambition," she said. "Not only will you learn how to control your bloodlust, but you're going to be one of the strongest, most powerful vampires alive. Besides myself, of course." She smiled, widening her eyes in a way that would have looked innocent if someone didn't know better.

"You didn't answer my question." I raised an eyebrow, unwilling to let her steer me off course so easily. "What happens to the vampires who can't control their bloodlust?"

"They're not allowed to live," she said simply. "At least, not the ones from our kingdom. And as *you're* a vampire of the Vale—a prince of it—our kingdom is all you need to concern yourself with right now."

"How many other kingdoms are there?" I asked.

"Six, including the Vale."

"And what are they like?"

"I'm here to oversee your transition—not to be a history teacher." She scrunched her nose, as if my question demeaned her. "The palace library is full of books with answers to those kind of questions."

"I'm allowed to leave my room?" Given my treatment since waking up, I hadn't expected as much.

"Of course," she said. "You're a prince, not a prisoner."

I was thrilled to hear this, but worried at the same time.

"What about the humans?" I asked, voicing the cause of my concern. "If I run into one and smell their blood, I might…" I trailed off, unable to say it out loud.

I might *murder* them.

"You won't run into any humans in the palace," she said. "The only humans here are in the dungeons."

"Humans don't work in the palace?"

"No." She laughed again. Clearly, she found my ignorance of life in the Vale amusing. "Humans are slaves. They give us their blood and do menial labor in exchange for their homes in the village at the outskirt of the kingdom. The respectable jobs—such as serving the nobility in the palace—are given to vampires. You'll only see other vampires in the palace, and your personal bodyguard will escort you everywhere you go."

"You're giving me a bodyguard?" I imagined it was to keep an eye on me rather than protect me.

"You met him earlier—he brought in the first human

for your transitional meal," she said. "His name is Daniel, and he's one of our best. I wouldn't give you anything but the best."

I nodded, feeling devoid of life as I took in everything from the past few hours.

None of this felt real. It felt like a bad dream—like I would wake up and everything would be back to normal again.

Neither of us spoke for nearly a full minute. Eventually she walked over to sit next to me, and she placed her hand on my leg.

I wanted to flinch away. But I just stared at where she was touching me, not moving.

Because with her this close to me, the needle full of wormwood was closer than ever.

If I got that needle, I could stab her with it and run.

But where would I go? The palace was full of vampires, and guards were outside my door. I guessed the guards had needles full of wormwood too.

I wouldn't make it five feet before they took me down. And that was all assuming that wormwood affected Laila at all.

"I know it's a lot to take in," she cooed. "But I'm here for you, for *anything* you need." She locked her eyes with mine, wet her lips, and leaned forward, her hand inching up my thigh.

Playing along would be a good way to gain her trust and improve my chance of escape.

But my stomach twisted with revulsion at the thought of being intimate with the woman who had stolen my life from me. Despite how beautiful she was on the outside, I only saw one thing when I looked at Laila now—a monster.

So I turned my head from her and leaned away.

Silence lingered in the air as she took in my refusal, and I flexed every muscle in my body, preparing for her to punish me with another dose of wormwood.

She drew her hand away from me, but she didn't reach for the needle.

"Fine." She spoke coolly, and she stood, staring down at me in disdain. "You don't have to want me romantically. But I'm your sire, which means we'll *always* be bound. I urge you not to forget that."

She turned around and left the room without giving me a chance to reply.

As the door slammed shut, I curled my hands into fists and swore that someday, she would regret ever choosing to turn me into a vampire prince.

9

JACEN

For the next week, I spent as much time as possible in the palace library, reading what I thought looked like the most important books in the non-fiction section. The texts were lengthy and wordy, especially the ones from centuries ago that were written in older forms of English. But I powered through them anyway.

Because to escape the Vale, I needed to know as much about the kingdom as possible.

I returned to my room at sunrise. As always, a large glass of blood waited for me on the table.

I downed the blood, but it wasn't enough. It was like I'd had an appetizer but no main course.

I needed *more*.

With the glass still in my hand, I marched to the door

and opened it. Daniel and another guard were in their positions outside my quarters.

"Your Highness?" Daniel's arms went to his sides as he stood to attention.

I'd never get used to that title. But what he called me was hardly a concern right now.

"I need more blood." I was quick to get to the point. "The amount I'm getting isn't enough."

"I understand." He stared straight ahead, not meeting my eyes. "I sent your complaint to the kitchens yesterday."

"And they gave me *less* today than they did yesterday!" My nerves felt like they'd reached a breaking point, and I threw the glass to the floor, shattering it in my fit of anger.

Daniel didn't flinch. "They're weaning you down to the point where you're satiated with a normal amount of blood each day," he repeated what he'd been telling me throughout the week. "You might feel like you need more blood than they're giving you, but you don't. That's your bloodlust talking—not your body. We've all been there before. The only way to overcome the bloodlust is to refrain from gorging yourself on blood you don't need."

"I'm not asking to *gorge* on blood." I grit my teeth together, not understanding why he didn't get it. Like he'd said, he'd been there before. He should understand. "I just need enough to function. One more pint a day. That's all I need."

I hated begging, but I was desperate. It was harder and harder to focus every day. Each day, I was inching closer to a breaking point.

"You're getting all you need." He finally met my gaze, surprising me with the worry in his eyes. "You need to learn to control yourself. If you don't… well, you know the rules as well as we all do."

Vampires who can't control their bloodlust aren't allowed to live.

It was the most important rule of the Vale. And if there was one major takeaway I'd had from my recent reading, it was that the supernaturals *loved* their many rules.

"Fine." I marched back into my room and slammed the door shut behind me. Daniel was only trying to help me—I knew that—but it didn't mean I had to like what he was saying.

I got ready for bed and tried to sleep, but it was impossible. As the week had progressed, falling asleep had been getting harder and harder. Now, all I could do was lay there, trying to think of ways to get more blood.

Despite what Daniel had told me, this had to be more

than my bloodlust talking. I *needed* more blood to function. I clearly wasn't being given enough.

Maybe Laila had taken my rejection of her advances harder than she'd made it seem? Maybe she was withholding blood from me as an act of revenge?

When hours passed and I still hadn't fallen asleep, I knew I only had one option. I'd have to go to Laila and beg her to understand. I'd do anything—literally *anything*—if she'd give me more blood.

If that meant taking her to bed, then so be it.

But it was noon—the middle of the night for vampires. If I woke Laila from her sleep, I'd only irritate her.

I'd have to wait until sunset.

For now, I raided the bar inside my quarters, finding the closest thing that resembled blood—a bottle of red wine. It looked like a fancy vintage, but I didn't care. After uncorking it, I didn't even bother pouring it into a glass. I drank it straight from the bottle.

It didn't take long until the bottle was empty.

I left the empty bottle on the table and pulled open the curtains to the doors that led to the balcony. I'd been in the palace for a week, and had yet to step outside. I'd spent the nighttime hours in the library, so I was only in my quarters was when the sun was up. And one of the first things I'd read about vampires was that while the sun didn't incinerate us on the spot, exposure to it was painful and draining. It was why vampires followed a nocturnal schedule.

Maybe if I stood in the sunlight for a few minutes, it would drain me of enough energy that I'd be able to sleep.

It would be painful. But at this point, I was willing to try anything for a few hours of sleep.

I opened the door to the balcony, and the sunlight poured through, so bright that it felt like I was looking directly at the sun. I blinked a few times, but that didn't stop the light from feeling like it was burning my retinas. I needed a seriously strong pair of sunglasses. But I didn't have any right now, so I forced myself to step out onto the balcony and into the sun.

As expected, it burned my skin. You know that feeling when you've been sitting outside for too long and you *know* you're going to have terrible sunburn? It was like that times ten. Every instinct in my body told me to go back inside, but I fought it. I even pushed up my sleeves, forcing myself to feel the sun against as much of my skin as possible. Forcing myself to endure the burn.

I *deserved* this pain after killing those people. I should make stepping out into the scorching sun a routine—a reminder of everyone who'd died because of me.

I walked to the railing and placed my hands down upon it, gazing out at the kingdom before me. Walls surrounded the perimeter of the palace. Right outside of them were the magnificent, ornate buildings that made up the vampire town. Empty merchant stalls were out on the main squares, and the streets were deserted, as the vampires were inside and likely asleep.

Beyond the magnificence of the town were the old, cracking buildings of the human village. The village was also quiet, as the humans kept the vampires' nocturnal schedule as well.

The entire kingdom was tucked between colossal mountains covered in powdery snow. The sky was a crystal clear blue overhead—it all came together to look like a perfect photo one might see on a postcard.

Come see the Canadian Rocky Mountains! Just watch out for the vampires who might bite you and kill you—or worse, turn you into a monster.

I didn't have time to chuckle at my terrible joke before a gust of wind blew from the mountains, bringing forward a smell that sent my senses on overdrive and coaxed my fangs out of my gums.

Human blood.

10

JACEN

A RED, filmy haze passed over my eyes. I *needed* that blood. And it was all there, in front of me for the taking.

So I was going to take it.

My room was too high up to jump, so I leaped from the balcony and scaled the wall down, careful not to get near any windows. I couldn't risk anyone spotting me.

If they spotted me, they might try to stop me. And if they stopped me, I'd continue to starve.

No one was going to stand in my way of that fresh, warm blood.

It didn't take long before I dropped down to the grass below, and I brushed myself off, hurrying to the wall surrounding the palace. However, unlike the stones that made up the exterior of the palace—the stones that allowed me to find placeholders for my hands and feet—this wall was made of smooth concrete. Climbing it was impossible, and it was too high to jump.

If my room had been at the back of the palace, I would have been home free, since the back of the palace made up the back of the wall. But of course, my room—a room for a prince of the Vale—was in front, over-looking the kingdom.

I supposed I'd have to leave the way everyone else did—through the front gate.

I glanced up at the open doors to my balcony, and something tugged at the back of my mind. A quiet voice telling me that the wall around the palace was there for a reason and that I should go back while I still could.

But I pushed the voice aside in favor of the tanta-lizing scent of human blood that had sent my senses buzzing. If I didn't get that blood, I would starve to death. Or go crazy. I was *already* going crazy. I wouldn't take much—not enough to kill. I'd only take enough to keep me satiated. Enough to make me feel *sane* again.

Laila had wanted me to learn to control my bloodlust.

Challenge accepted.

I followed the wall to the entrance. Four guards stood at alert, under a covered awning to stay out of the sun. They wore clothing that covered nearly every part of their skin, and sunglasses over their eyes. Gleaming swords were strapped to each one of their sides.

"Prince Jacen." The guard closest to me—the only woman of the four—recognized me in a heartbeat. "You're not allowed to leave the palace. Queen Laila's orders."

She and the other guards lined up along the entrance, creating a barrier between the town and me. But they didn't reach for their swords. Thanks to the reading I'd been doing in the library, I knew why. The vampires of the Vale were *very* intense about their royal hierarchy. They wouldn't raise a hand against me—a prince—unless absolutely necessary.

I itched to run past them to get to the humans as quickly as possible. But the moment I stepped outside the palace walls, I'd be going against Queen Laila's orders and they'd have the right to attack. I was strong, but I didn't have the fighting experience to go against four trained guards.

However, since I was a royal, there was one thing I had that they didn't.

Compulsion.

I didn't know how to use compulsion—I'd never tried before. But it was my best chance to get to those humans, so now was as good of a time as ever to try.

"Queen Laila changed her mind." I focused on how

desperate I was to get to that human blood and forced every bit of determination and willpower into my voice as possible, looking at each of them as I spoke. "You will let me pass, and you'll mention this encounter to no one. And you." I looked at the guard wearing a sleek pair of Oakley sunglasses. "You're going to give me your glasses. And your hat."

Yes, my original purpose of coming outside was to torture myself by sunlight. But now that I had a greater purpose—getting to that human blood—I needed as much protection against the sun as possible.

He removed his sunglasses and hat and handed them to me, his eyes dazed.

I couldn't see the others' eyes behind their glasses, but they all stepped to the side, giving me room to pass.

My compulsion had worked.

But I didn't have time to marvel over this new discovery. Because that blood was waiting, and the more time I wasted, the hungrier I became.

So I put on the hat and sunglasses and rushed through the vampire town toward the human village, following the scent that called to me like a siren's song— the human blood.

11

JACEN

A FEW MORE GUARDS STOPPED ME in the vampire town, but they were as easy to compel as the ones at the palace. Still, I kept to the edge of town, so I'd run into as little trouble as possible.

As I ran, the smell of the blood grew stronger and stronger, until I crossed the invisible line to enter the ramshackle human village.

The glorious scent of warm blood surrounded me, wafting through the tiny windows that had been open to let in the crisp winter air.

I zeroed in on the nearest building and ran toward it. The door was locked, but the lock was cheap—it was clearly meant to keep out humans, not vampires. With my strength, I forced it open without a problem, barely making a sound.

The building was some sort of laundry facility—the first floor was filled with washers and driers. There wasn't a soul around. But my body was working on instinct now, and I headed straight to where the scent of blood was coming from—the stairs.

I ran upstairs, staying light on my feet so I didn't wake anyone up, and... jackpot.

It was a room full of bunk beds, with women sleeping on each bunk.

Now that I was in the same room as the humans, the red haze of bloodlust took over completely. I needed blood, and I needed as *much* of it as possible. The blood sang to me, urging me to stop fighting what I'd become and to take what I needed.

Fighting wasn't worth the hunger, the anxiety, and the sleepless nights. I was strong, I was an immortal, and I wouldn't let Laila deprive me of the blood I needed.

Rage consumed me at the thought of the deceptive queen, and I ran for the closest woman, smiling and sinking my fangs into her neck.

My body buzzed with pleasure the moment her sweet, delicious blood hit my tongue. *This* was what I was meant to have been drinking the entire time I'd been in the Vale. The bottled stuff had nothing on blood fresh from the vein.

But I barely had a taste of it before the woman

screamed and pushed at me. Instantly, the other women in the room to woke up and started screaming, too.

They needed to *shut up*.

I threw the woman to the ground and turned around, ready to compel the others into submission. But one of them was already heading toward the stairs, and another was running at me with a stake.

They didn't seriously think they could pull one over on me, did they?

I circled the room in seconds, breaking each woman's neck before they had a chance to realize what was happening. They were weak, vulnerable, and pathetic. They were *prey*.

They should have thought twice before trying to attack the predator.

Once they were all dead, I returned to the original woman, eager to continue my meal. But her eyes stared blankly ahead—dead.

I shook her, as if that could wake her up, but of course it did nothing. I leaned back and grunted in frustration. This was the only woman in the building whose neck I *hadn't* broken. I'd been sure not to break it, since I'd wanted her alive.

So why was she dead? There were no obvious trauma marks on her body.

But then I turned her around and saw that the back of her head was bashed in.

I must have used so much force when I'd thrown her to the floor that the impact had smashed in her skull. Now her blood wasn't even *halfway* as appealing as it had been when her heart had been beating.

I scrunched my nose in disgust and tossed her corpse to the floor. All that trouble, and I'd only gotten a sip. One measly sip. I could still taste the blood on my tongue, and it was torturing me—making me even thirstier than before.

I ran out of the building and headed to the closest one across the street, easily pushing through the flimsy lock on the door. Again, I made sure to be quiet—the humans inside couldn't know I was coming.

It was clear from the giant aluminum casings and elaborate piping inside that I'd entered a distillery. The air inside was warm, smelling like hops and wheat. But those scents paled compared to what I'd come here for —human blood.

Like the other building, the smell of the blood came from the second floor. I ran upstairs and found another room full of bunks. But unlike the last building, this one was full of men, not women.

Just like before, I whizzed around the room, breaking their necks before they had a chance to fight or scream. Unlike before, I stopped when there was one man left standing.

He was middle aged, with a balding head and a beer belly that hung over the top of his pants. He smelled like beer, but then again, *everything* in this building smelled like beer. His eyes were full of fear, and his lips trembled as he looked at me.

I expected him to beg for his life, but he said nothing.

"Say nothing, and don't fight me." I pushed compulsion into my voice, giddy with anticipation as the hypnosis took hold and his eyes glazed over. Then I smiled and sank my fangs into his fleshy neck, ready for the delicious gush of fresh blood.

Instead of the sweetness I'd been anticipating, I got a soured, fermented gulp. His blood tasted like warm beer that had been sitting out for a few days too long.

I ripped my fangs out of his flesh and spat out what I had yet to swallow. "You're drunk," I accused, wiping my lips to get rid of the disgusting taste.

He simply smiled and shrugged sheepishly, laughing without making a sound.

Anger exploded through my veins, and I clenched my hands into fists by my sides. He thought this was *funny*? I'd show him what was funny. Because I hadn't come all this way and killed so many people to drink bitter, tainted blood. I was going to have my feast, and I was going to do it right.

Which meant I had no more time to waste on this drunken, bumbling idiot.

So I growled at him and snapped his neck, dropping his corpse to the floor before continuing on my way.

12

JACEN

WHEN I RE-ENTERED THE STREET, lights were starting to go on in some of the buildings. But the sun was still out —it was far too early for anyone to rise.

I must have created enough noise to stir the humans.

I couldn't have them wandering around and finding me while I fed. As I'd discovered in the first building— the laundry facility—I was vulnerable while feeding. I'd known to pull away from my meal back then because those women had started screaming. If they'd been stealthier, they could have staked me in the back while I'd been lost in the pleasure of drinking blood, killing me in an instant.

I'd been lucky that time, but I wouldn't make the same mistake again.

The only thing more important than drinking blood was staying alive.

I ran to the end of the road and turned the corner to the edge of the village, finding a cabin next to a chicken coop. It was perfect—far enough away from the section that had started to wake that I could feed undisturbed.

This time I did it right, killing all of the people inside with one fell swoop and leaving one of them alive to feed from. Her blood was perfect—as sweet as expected—and I only let go once I'd drained her dry.

But it wasn't enough. I was still hungry. I needed *more*.

There was another cabin next door, so I barged inside it and did the same thing there.

I'd just dropped the corpse to the floor when terrified eyes peeked out from the crawlspace above. They belonged to a young boy who looked no older than twelve. I must have been so consumed in my urge to feed that I hadn't thought to check the overhead space. I'd just assumed it was empty.

Now it held one more human whose blood was mine for the taking.

I couldn't believe I'd missed him earlier. His blood smelled pure—cleaner than any of the others. Perhaps it was because he was a child.

I launched myself up to the crawlspace, licking my lips as I stalked toward him. This was going to be tasty.

"Vampires are supposed to protect us." The boy held his hands up and backed away, his eyes wide in terror. "Not hurt us."

But I wasn't listening to him. All I could hear was the thumping of his heart as it pumped his blood through his veins. His scent was so intoxicating that I was already imagining how delicious it would taste the moment it touched my tongue.

I jumped on him and sank my fangs into his neck, thrilled to find that his blood tasted as good as it smelled. If there was a delicacy amongst blood, child's blood was surely it.

Unfortunately, I didn't get to finish drinking from him before a needle pricked my neck, injecting me with so much wormwood that I passed out on the spot.

13

JACEN

I SUCKED IN A SHARP BREATH, my heart racing as I jolted awake.

I was back in my bed in the palace. A woman stood over me—thin, with brown hair and average features. She wore a long necklace with a green gemstone, the color standing out against her all-black outfit.

She pulled something away—a needle—and placed it on the nightstand.

"Who are you?" I sat up in bed, wiping cold sweat off my forehead. "What did you do to me?"

"My name is Camelia," she said. "I'm the witch of the Vale."

I knew all about the existence of witches—I'd read about them in the library. There weren't many witches left, especially strong ones. Most of them had been killed in the Great Supernatural War in the early twentieth century.

The Vale only had six witches. One main witch to maintain the boundary—the strongest witch in the kingdom—and five lesser strength witches in case something happened to the main witch. All of the witches in the Vale were female, as Laila didn't want them breeding without her consent.

"You maintain the boundary around the kingdom," I assumed, since she'd called herself *the* witch of the Vale. "And you act as Laila's second in command."

"I've heard you've been quite the eager student." She tilted her head, sizing me up. "Impressive."

"What did you give me?" I glanced at the empty needle, not wanting to dance around my original question. I felt different than I had yesterday—*fuller*—and I assumed it was thanks to whatever she'd shot me up with.

"An antidote to the wormwood you received in the village." She fiddled with the needle and smiled, as if proud of what it had contained. "You did a good job compelling those guards. Laila was impressed—no new vampire has ever mastered compulsion so quickly. But of course, everywhere in the kingdom is equipped with alarm systems—even the human village. You didn't think you were going to get away with that stunt without getting caught, did you?"

"What?" I sat up straighter, surprised again by how *satiated* I felt. My body ached because of the wormwood —it felt like my muscles had been shredded to pieces and then stitched back together—but for the first time in a long time, I wasn't dying of thirst.

I hadn't felt so full since Laila had supplied me with all of those humans to feed from right after I was turned.

"Do you remember what happened last night?" Camelia raised an eyebrow, and she scooted closer when she apparently realized that no, I didn't remember. "When suffering extreme bloodlust, it can take a while for the memories of what the vampire did during their haze to return." She spoke faster, clearly excited by this fact. "You went on quite the spree—it was the worst we've ever seen. If you need assistance remembering, I can do my best to help you out…"

Her mention of "bloodlust" and a "spree" slowly brought the memories to the surface, and I stared blankly at the wall as I remembered the horrific things I'd done while the majority of the kingdom had been sleeping.

From the moment I'd gotten a whiff of the human

blood from the village, it was like something had taken over my soul, possessing me. *Making* me attack those humans in their sleep in a desperate hunt for their blood.

I didn't want to believe it. How could I have done such awful things?

Except that it *had* been me. Every last second of it. It was all my fault.

I hadn't been possessed by anything except my own bloodlust.

That bloodlust would always be a part of me. A demon lurking in the back of my mind, urging me to kill.

I was going to go to Hell for this. And I damned well deserved it.

"Why am I still alive?" I rubbed the back of my neck where I'd been shot with wormwood last night. "By the rules of the Vale, Laila should have killed me already."

I *wanted* her to kill me. I had no right to live after taking so many lives.

"Laila is giving you a second chance," Camelia said.

"What?" In what I'd read so far about the Vale, no vampire who'd lost control of his or her bloodlust had *ever* been given a second chance. If you lost control, you were killed. That was the rule. "Why?"

"Because apparently, the all-mighty queen made a mistake." Camelia smirked—I wasn't sure if she was amused, or if she didn't believe it herself. "She underestimated how much blood you needed per day to wean you down to a normal amount. You're stronger than she ever imagined. Your excellent use of compulsion against all those guards showed us as much. Not to mention how viciously you tore through that village…" She smiled again, like my power excited her.

But I didn't *want* this power. I'd rather be dead.

Perhaps that was why I'd gone on my rampage in the first place. Because I knew that by doing something so horrible, I wouldn't be allowed to live.

"If Laila won't kill me, then you should." I gazed at Camelia, putting as much compulsion into my tone as I could manage. I was weaker due to the wormwood in my system, but thanks to the antidote, I could still tap into the magic. "It's the law of the Vale. You know it as well as I. So do it. Kill me. Now."

"Trying to use compulsion on me?" Camelia threw her head back and laughed. "Save it. Don't you know that witches of the Vale are the only citizens allowed to wear wormwood as protection?" She caressed the green amulet that hung from her neck as if it were a child instead of an ugly piece of jewelry.

"I suppose I've yet to reach that part in my reading," I quipped.

"Well, now you know," she said. "And Laila has

compelled the vampire guards not to harm you. As your sire and your *queen*, her compulsion is stronger than yours, so don't try that stunt on them too. Laila wants you alive, so you can bet you're going to stay that way."

"Why are you even here?" I sighed and leaned back into the bed. "Did Laila send you to make sure I remembered what I did? If so, then mission accomplished. You're free to leave now."

"That was the first thing I needed to do," she said. "But no—there's much, much more to it then that."

I crossed my arms and stared at her, wanting her to get out with it.

"I gave you the antidote right now for a reason." She stood and looked at me over her shoulder, motioning for me to follow her into the living room. "Come. There's an official Vale broadcast happening soon that Laila insisted you watch."

14

JACEN

I FOLLOWED Camelia into the living room, and she picked up the remote, pressing the button that brought the television down from the ceiling.

But I couldn't focus on the television once noticing that the balcony doors were now sealed with a massive, hard-core padlock.

"That's a military grade lock," Camelia said, following my gaze. "It's the best on the market. There are two of them—one inside the doors and one outside. Not even *you* will be able to get through that. And all the windows in the palace are hurricane-proof, unbreakable by even the strongest supernaturals."

"So I'm a prisoner." I'd feared it from the moment I'd arrived here.

Now these locks were making it official.

"You won't be leaving the palace until you're in control of your bloodlust. But if you were a prisoner, you'd be in the dungeons," Camelia repeated what Laila had said when I'd asked her the same thing a few days ago. "This is simply an extra precaution to protect the humans. We need them alive to keep our kingdom efficiently running. The royal vampires have used compulsion to relax them after the stir you caused in the village, but restocking the ones you killed is going to be quite the hassle."

She said it so naturally—as if referring to people like they were animals was normal. She—and *all* of the supernaturals in the Vale—disgusted me.

She disgusted me so much that I couldn't bring myself to deign her with a reply.

"Now you need to focus," she chided. "Like I said, there's a special Vale broadcast that Laila wants you to see." She situated herself on the sofa and patted the seat next to her, giving me a "come hither" look.

Gross. She must be deluded to think I'd ever be interested in her.

I crossed my arms and remained where I was.

"Or stand, if you prefer." She pouted like a child who'd been told no at a candy store, although she got a hold of herself a second later. "All that matters is that you watch."

She inputted the channel, and the image on the screen switched to one of Laila standing on a platform in the center of the main square in town. The queen wore a long, red dress—she looked like she belonged in a period drama—and she had a golden crown perched on her head.

Next to Laila was a disgruntled man with cuffs around his wrists and ankles. His height and build were similar to mine, although his hair was a few shades lighter. He refused to look at the surrounding crowd, instead just staring at his feet in shame.

"There are only vampires in the crowd," I observed, noticing that all of the people shown on the broadcast wore expensive, fine clothing—clothes that only vampires could afford to purchase.

"Humans are watching from the televisions in the village," Camelia said. "They're not allowed to mix with the vampires."

"The humans have televisions?"

"Only to watch official Vale broadcasts," she said. "Their televisions are blocked from watching anything else. Now—pay attention. This is important."

I turned my attention back to the broadcast. The

man in shackles shuffled his feet, still refusing to look up.

"Thank you, fine citizens of the Vale, for gathering here today," Laila said. The crowd grew silent at her words, all eyes on her. "As you all now know, yesterday we experienced one of the worst massacres in the history of the Vale. Nearly one hundred of our humans —the humans we've all sworn to shelter and protect— were victims to a newly turned vampire who lost control of his bloodlust. This goes against everything we stand for, and it will *not* be permitted!"

The crowd screamed out in agreement, many of them raising their fists in support.

"The vampire next to me—John Morley—is responsible for this brutal attack," she continued. "Due to the extremity of his crime, I've brought him up with me today to demonstrate what happens when a vampire of the Vale breaks our rules." She turned to gaze at the man, her eyes dark and serious. "Do you, John Morley, plead guilty to massacring nearly one hundred humans in their sleep last night?" she asked.

"Yes." His voice was monotone, and he finally turned his eyes up to the camera—they were wide with fear. "I do."

Outcries broke out from the crowd.

"But that man didn't do it." I stared at the television in disbelief. "I did."

"I know that." Camelia smirked again. "Laila knows as well."

"So why's he taking the blame for *my* crime?"

"Because Laila compelled him to do so," she said. "Just like she compelled the guards who saw you to believe they'd seen John and not you. As for the humans, the only ones who saw you up close are now dead. And for those who got a glimpse of you from far away, the sunglasses and hat you wore made you practically indistinguishable from John. In comparison to other bumps the Vale has hit along the centuries, this cover up was relatively simple."

Time felt like it stood still around me. I didn't think I could feel any more guilt than I'd felt after killing all those humans.

It turned out I was wrong.

"It should be me up there." I glanced at my padlocked door, wishing I could run out there with the truth to put a stop to this myself. "Not him."

"The queen sees great potential in you," Camelia said. "She spent a lot of time browsing through potential princes before selecting you. She's not willing to let you go just yet."

With that, she turned back to the screen, refocusing on the broadcast.

The crowd continued to scream out against the man, until Laila finally raised a hand to silence them.

"Thank you for your confession." Laila's voice was hard and cold. "Now, you must pay the price for your crime."

She held her hand out to the side, and a guard handed her a silver stake. With swift precision, she arced the stake around in a deadly blow to John's heart.

John's eyes went wide, glazing over a second later.

She pulled out the stake and he tumbled backward, hitting the platform floor like a piece of wood. Laila didn't bother looking at him. Instead, she raised the stake to her mouth, slowly licking off the blood coating its end.

Vampire blood tasted bland to vampires, and it offered us no nourishment.

She was doing this for show.

Having seen enough, I ripped the remote from Camelia's hand and pressed pause. The broadcast stopped right after Laila had finished licking the stake, a smug smile on the queen's face.

I *hated* her more than I'd hated anyone in my life. She couldn't continue getting away with this. Keeping humans as slaves, turning people into vampires against their will… it was wrong. Not to mention all the others who had died because they'd gotten in the way of her plans, like my teammates and all the other innocent lives that had been lost in the bombing she'd orchestrated at the hotel.

She'd destroyed too many lives, and she needed to be stopped.

It was at that moment, as I stared into Laila's eyes on the television screen, that I made a vow. I'd play her game for now. I'd continue to learn as much as possible about the supernatural world. I'd get control over my bloodlust. I'd learn proper combat skills under the pretense of wanting to protect the Vale and everyone in it no matter what.

I'd become the model prince that Laila desired.

Then, once I had her unconditional trust, I'd kill the vampire queen who had destroyed my life and the lives of so many others. Nothing could make up for the lives I'd taken, but killing her would be a good start. It might take a while—years, or perhaps longer than that—but I was an immortal now. I'd be patient until it was the perfect time to strike.

Because I wouldn't rest until Queen Laila was dead.

I hope you enjoyed The Vampire Rules! The series continues in The Vampire Wish, the first book in the Dark World: The Vampire Wish series. Go to myBook.to/vampirewishpaperback to grab The Vampire Wish now, or turn the page for a sneak peak of the first few chapters!

PROLOGUE: ANNIKA

"RACE YOU TO THE BOTTOM!" my older brother Grant yelled the moment we got off the chair lift.

Mom and Dad skied up ahead, but beyond the four of us, the rest of the mountain was empty. It was the final run of the trip, on our last day of spring break, and we'd decided to challenge ourselves by skiing down the hardest trail on the mountain—one of the double black diamond chutes in the back bowl.

The chutes were the only way down from where we were—the chairlift that took us up here specified that these trails were for experts only. Which was perfect for us. After all, I'd been skiing since I was four years old. My parents grew up skiing, and they couldn't wait to get me and Grant on the trails. We could tackle any trail at this ski resort.

"Did I hear something about a race?" Dad called from up ahead.

"Damn right you did!" Grant lifted one of his poles in the air and hooted, ready to go.

"You're on." I glided past all of them, the thrill of competition already racing through my veins.

Mom pleaded with us to be careful, and then my skis tipped over the top of the mountain, and I was flying down the trail.

I smiled as I took off. I'd always wanted to fly, but obviously that wasn't possible, and skiing was the closest thing I'd found to that. If I lived near a mountain instead of in South Florida, I might have devoted my extracurricular activities to skiing instead of gymnastics.

I blazed down the mountain like I was performing a choreographed dance, taking each jump with grace and digging my poles into the snow with each turn. This trail was full of moguls and even some rocky patches, but I flew down easily, avoiding each obstacle as it approached. I loved the rush of the wind on my cheeks and the breeze through my hair. If I held my poles in the air, it really *did* feel like flying.

I was lost in the moment—so lost that I didn't see the patch of rocks ahead until it was too late. I wasn't prepared for the jump, and instead of landing gracefully,

I ploofed to the ground, wiping out so hard that both of my skis popped off of my boots.

"Wipeout!" Grant laughed, holding his poles up in the air and flying past me.

"Are you okay?" Mom asked from nearby.

"Yeah, I'm fine." I rolled over, locating my skis. One was next to me, the other a few feet above.

"Do you need help?" she asked.

"No." I shook my head, brushing the snow off my legs. "I've got this. Go on. I'll meet you all at the bottom."

She nodded and continued down the mountain, knowing me well enough to understand that I didn't need any help—I wanted to get back up on my own. "See you there!" she said, taking the turns slightly more cautiously than Grant and Dad.

I trudged up the mountain to grab the first ski, popped it back on, and glided on one foot to retrieve the other. I huffed as I prepared to put it back on. What an awful final run of the trip. My family was nearing the bottom of the trail—there was no way I would catch up with them now.

Looked like I would be placing last in our little race. Which annoyed me, because last place was *so* not my style.

But I still had to get down, so I took a deep breath, dug my poles into the snow, and set off.

As I was nearing the bottom, three men emerged from the forest near the end of the chute. None of them wore skis, and they were dressed in jeans, t-shirts, and leather jackets. They must have been freezing.

I stopped, about to call out and ask them if they needed help. But before I could speak, one of them moved in a blur, coming up behind my brother and sinking his teeth into his neck.

I screamed as Grant's blood gushed from the wound, staining the snow red.

The other two men moved just as fast, one of them pouncing on my mom, the other on my dad. More blood gushed from both of their necks, their bodies limp like rag dolls in their attackers arms.

"No!" I flew down the mountain—faster than I'd ever skied before—holding my poles out in front of me. I reached my brother first and jammed the pole into the back of his attacker with as much force I could muster.

The pole bounced off the man, not even bothering him in the slightest, and the force of the attack pushed me to the ground. All I could do was look helplessly up as the man dropped my brother into the blood stained snow.

What was going on? Why were they *doing* this?

Then his gaze shifted to me, and he stared me down.

His eyes were hard and cold—and he snarled at me, baring his teeth.

They were covered in my brother's blood.

"Grant," I whispered my brother's name, barely able to speak. He was so pale—so still. And there so much blood. The rivulets streamed from the puddles around him, the glistening redness so bright that it seemed fake against the frosty background.

One of the other men dropped my mom's body on the ground next to my brother. Seconds later, my dad landed next to them.

My mother's murderer grabbed first man's shoulder —the man who had murdered my brother. "Hold it, Daniel," he said, stopping him from moving toward me.

I just watched them, speechless. My whole family was gone. These creatures ran faster than I could blink, and they were strong enough to handle bodies like they were weightless.

I had no chance at escape.

They were going to do this to me too, weren't they? These moments—right here, right now—would be my last.

I'd never given much thought to what happens after people die. Who does, at eighteen years old? I was supposed to have my whole life ahead of me.

My *family* was supposed to have their whole lives ahead of them, too.

Now their lifeless, bloody bodies at the bottom of this mountain would be the last things I would ever see.

I steadied myself, trying to prepare for what was coming. Would dying hurt? Would it be over quickly? Would I disappear completely once I was gone? Would my soul continue on, or would my existence be wiped from the universe forever?

It wasn't supposed to be this way. I didn't want to die. I wanted to *live.*

But I'd seen what those men—those *creatures*—had done to my family. And I knew, staring up at them, that it was over.

Terror filled my body, shaking me to the core. I couldn't fight them. I couldn't win. Against them, I was helpless.

And even if I stood a chance, did I really want to continue living while my family was gone?

"We can't kill them all," the man continued. "Laila sent us here to get humans to replace the ones that rabid vampire killed in his bloodlust rampage. We need to keep her alive."

"I suppose she'll do." The other man glared down at me, licking his lips and clenching his fists. "It's hard to tell under all that ski gear, but she looks pretty. She'll make a good addition to the Vale."

He took a syringe out of his jacket, ran at me in a blur, and jabbed the needle into my neck.

The empty, dead eyes of my parents were the last things I saw before my head hit the snow and everything went dark.

1: JACEN

ONE YEAR LATER

THE SCREAMS. The hunger. The blood.

I'd never forget the terrified looks on each of my victim's faces as I'd sunk my fangs into their necks and drained the lives from their bodies.

They haunted my dreams since the massacre. I relived it every night. The lust for their blood—the scent of it so tantalizingly delicious that my entire body burned for it, my fangs pushing through my gums and craving the silky feeling of the warm, smooth blood flowing down my throat. The way my soul parted with my mind as it gave into the craving—the desire for more and more until I'd consumed so much blood that every inch of my body was bloated and bursting with it.

It had been nearly a year since the massacre, and the

nightmares hadn't stopped. I didn't think they ever would.

I would never forgive myself for the pain and heartbreak I'd caused that night when I lost control of my bloodlust and slaughtered those humans in the village. So many of them had died that Queen Laila had to send out troops to replenish their stock.

Stock. As if they were crates of meat, or animals waiting to be slaughtered.

In my dreams, I saw the face of my final victim—the young boy who must have been no older than twelve. Then I woke up with a sharp breath, my fangs out and my gums aching for blood.

As always, a glass of it waited on my nightstand.

I reached for it, downing it in nearly one gulp. It tasted bitter—refrigerated blood always did—but it satisfied the craving enough that after a few deep breaths, I was able to pull my fangs back up into my gums and keep them there.

Still, my body craved more. But I didn't *need* more—I just *wanted* it. The craving was in my mind. It was an addiction—it wasn't real. What I'd just consumed was enough to sustain me for the rest of the day.

The blood I craved was my greatest desire and my greatest enemy.

After first turning, the lust for it controlled my every

thought. But as the days had passed—slowly but surely—I'd improved at controlling my cravings. Three glasses in the morning eventually became two, and then became one.

Still, Laila refused to let me leave the palace. Not until I could prove that I could control my bloodlust around humans. After all, she couldn't have me killing any more of them. Not after the *inconvenience* I'd caused a year ago when I'd lost myself to that bloodlust filled haze.

Never mind the *inconvenience* she'd caused me by turning me into a vampire against my will.

And while I was strong, I wasn't strong enough to take down a group of guards on my own.

It was hard to believe it had only been a year ago that I'd been a human, unaware of the existence of supernaturals at all. After being locked in this palace for all that time, that year felt like an eternity.

This extravagant palace hidden in the wilderness of the Canadian Rockies—in an enchanted valley that the vampires called the Vale—had become my prison. Every day, I was suffocating. I needed to get out.

Which was why I'd been working daily on controlling my bloodlust. And slowly but surely, I'd been getting better.

Now, I placed the glass down on my nightstand and

looked out my window as the last rays of the sun sunk over the horizon. I took deep, measured breaths, and the craving disappeared, my veins cooling down entirely.

I smiled, knowing this was it. I was ready to prove that I'd gained control of the monstrous creature I'd become.

I was ready to be free.

2: JACEN

"YOUR HIGHNESS," my vampire guard Daniel said as he stepped inside my room.

I didn't think I would ever get used to being called that. After all, I was no prince. As a human, I'd been an eager swimmer, ready to conquer my first Olympics and get gold medals in as many categories as possible.

That person had died the moment Laila sank her fangs into my neck and damned me to an eternity of hell.

Daniel glanced at the empty glass on my nightstand, no hint of emotion flickering across his eyes. "Would you like another glass of blood?" he asked.

"No." I walked over to the window, observing the nearby village. Lights were starting to flicker on in the small houses the humans lived in. Just as I, they were preparing to start their day. Well, *night*, since we operated on a nocturnal schedule in the Vale.

I turned back to face Daniel. "I would like to speak with Queen Laila," I said.

He pressed his lips together, saying nothing. "Is it an important matter?" he finally asked. "As you know, the queen just returned from visiting the Carpathian Kingdom, and she has to catch up on everything she missed in her absence."

"It's important." I held his gaze with his, flexing my arms by my sides. "I'm ready."

"For what?" he asked.

"To put myself in the presence of a human."

Laila entered my room thirty minutes later, her trusted witch advisor Camelia following obediently behind her.

Camelia, as always, wore a glass pendant around her neck with a piece of wormwood inside. As a witch, she was one of the only mortals in the kingdom allowed to use wormwood to protect herself. Laila wore a short, flowing blue dress, and her raven colored hair flowed behind her, making her look more like a teen Hollywood starlet than a centuries year old monster.

She was the worst kind of monster—the kind you never saw coming.

I sure hadn't.

On the night I'd met her in a bar, all I was thinking was that she was a beautiful girl, and that I wanted nothing more than to bring her back to my hotel room and see how far she was willing to go with me.

If someone had told me what she *really* was, I would have laughed in their face.

Because Laila wasn't just an ordinary vampire. She was one of the *original* vampires.

There had been seven of them in all. All part of a cult of witches who were so determined to stay young and beautiful forever that they'd created a spell using dark magic to make them exactly what they'd wanted —immortal.

None of them knew it would turn them into monsters. At least, that's what the six living originals claimed.

But I didn't believe it. Because none of them seemed to hate what they were. In fact, they seemed to *relish* in it.

"Jacen," Laila said my name, the slight lilt in her accent the only evidence that she wasn't from this place and time. "Are you sure you're ready?"

"Especially after what happened last time," Camelia added with a smirk.

As always, the green-eyed witch loved to taunt me. I knew she was referring to four months ago—the last time I tried to drink from a human. They hadn't been able to bring him through the door before I'd caught a whiff of his scent and lost myself to the haze of my bloodlust.

The next thing I'd known, I was staring at his corpse on the ground, the last bits of his blood dripping off my fangs and onto the polished marble floor by my feet.

"I suppose the loss of one human won't be too big of a deal." Camelia waved her hand and turned to Laila. "But of course, the decision is yours, Your Highness."

Laila eyed me up thoughtfully, tilting her head and softly biting her blood red lip. "The loss of one human would be irrelevant," she confirmed. "Daniel—go fetch one from the dungeons. An old one, who wouldn't be much use to us anyway."

Daniel rushed out of the room in a blur, returning ten minutes later dragging a thin, older man with a chain. "Sit," he commanded the man, throwing him onto the nearest armchair.

The man cowered in the chair and curled up into a ball, shaking and not looking up at any of us.

I smelled his blood—the rich, thick liquid pulsing

through his veins, and it was so tempting that my fangs itched to protrude. His jugular pulsed and pulsed, calling me closer.

But I swallowed down the urge, forcing my breaths to become shallow. I could control myself. I *had* to control myself.

It was the only way to prove that I was able to leave the palace.

"Very good." Laila nodded after a full minute had passed.

"That's it?" I asked her. "Are we done here?"

"No." She pressed her lips together, mischief dancing in her bright blue eyes. "You've only proven that you can be *around* a human."

"Isn't that what I needed to prove?" I asked. "That I can be around them without losing control?"

"You're a vampire prince." She ran a finger along one of my arms and pulled away, smiling sinfully. "Your stamina needs to be stronger than that."

"How so?" I clenched my fists tighter, ignoring her touch. Instead, I stared at the man's neck again, dreading her next words.

"I want you to drink from him."

3: JACEN

"You want me to kill him?" I kept my gaze on hers, unwilling to look at the human in question.

"No." The smug smile remained on her deceivingly innocent face. "I want you to drink from him and to control yourself. I want you to pull away *before* killing him. To enjoy your meal and leave him alive."

"I don't think I can do that." I stared her down, since she must know I was right. She was asking me to do this because she wanted me to kill him.

I shouldn't have expected anything less from her.

The vampire queen *looked* young and innocent, but her soul was dark and twisted.

"You can do it," she said simply. "As a great scientist once said—if you put your mind to it, you can accomplish anything."

"That's not a real scientist." I glared at her. "It's a quote from a movie."

"That's irrelevant." She waved my point away. "The point is that it's the truth. You're a vampire now, Jacen. The strongest of all species."

Camelia gave a small huff, but Laila ignored her.

"When I turned you last year, I gave you a gift," Laila continued.

"A gift I never wanted."

"Nevertheless, I gave it to you," she said. "You're a vampire prince now, Jacen. Show me that you deserve the title."

"And if I don't?" I challenged.

"You do." She laughed, light and melodic. "You may not see it now, but you will. Someday, you will. But for now—feed from him."

I eyed up the human man. How did he get in the prison? How old was he? Did he have a family?

I couldn't ask in front of Laila and Camelia. They viewed the human blood slaves as animals instead of people. Angering them would get me nowhere.

Instead, I created answers to the questions to myself. I imagined that this man had a family—a newborn grandchild he was excited to get to know. That he wanted his family to have more food than their rations allowed, since the rations only afforded bare survival for the humans. So he stole—bread from the vampires. The bread that vampires didn't even *need* to eat to survive, but enjoyed anyway, simply because they could. He got caught, and was unfairly locked in the dungeons, doomed to become a personal blood slave for the vampires in the palace—doomed to have them drink and drink from him until he died of blood loss and his remains were fed to the wolves outside the enchanted boundaries.

I looked into his eyes, trying to convince myself that this story I'd created for him was true.

Humanizing him might be the difference between if I was able to stop myself from losing myself to the bloodlust or if I killed him.

"Are you ready?" Laila sighed and tapped her foot impatiently. "We don't have all day."

"I'm ready." I stared at the man—examining his wrinkled face and reminding myself of the story I'd created.

I wouldn't kill him.

I would let him live.

I inched toward him and lowered myself down, my fangs sliding out of my gums as the scent of his blood filled my nose. Then my teeth sunk into his flesh and I was gulping down the warm, fresh blood.

How had I thought that the bitter, refrigerated blood could compare? How had I convinced myself that I could live off that garbage for the rest of my immortal existence? Noble vampires in the Vale were afforded the luxury of drinking straight from humans—I should *enjoy* the indulgence, not cower away from it.

It wasn't like I had much else to look forward to anymore. Not after my mortal life—my *soul*—had been taken from me against my will.

If the intoxicating taste of fresh blood was all I could enjoy, then so be it.

Just when I was beginning to enjoy myself, the blood supply stopped. I sucked deeper on his neck, trying to will out the final drops, and I squeezed his arms harder, as if that could push out more blood.

But there was nothing left.

He was drained dry.

4: CAMELIA

I LOVED WATCHING JACEN FEED.

Ever since he'd been brought to the palace, I'd been fascinated by the vampire prince—the handsome swimmer I'd advised that Laila turn after her previous prince had been driven mad by the bloodlust and had sacrificed himself to the wolves.

As Jacen drained the old man, I reached for the pendant I always wore around my neck—the one filled with wormwood—stroking it and holding my breath. I watched as the man stopped struggling, as his hands went limp, and as his head eventually rolled to the side, his eyes empty and dead.

As predicted, Jacen had lost control again. Consumed by his bloodlust. It wasn't surprising.

Because the stronger the vampire, the harder it was for them to control their urge to drain humans dry.

Jacen was shaping up to become one of the most powerful vampires that ever existed.

And I was determined to make him mine.

"Take the body away," Laila told Daniel, barely glancing at the drained corpse.

Jacen didn't tear his eyes away from the old man as Daniel heaved him over his shoulder and walked out of the room.

"You're not ready," Laila told Jacen sharply. "In time you will be, but not yet."

"How do I control it?" he asked her—begged her. "Why don't I know when to stop?"

"You're improving," Laila said. "The fact that you didn't maul him the moment you smelled his blood was significant progress. But you need more time."

"How much more?"

"There's no exact formula," she said. "It will happen when you want it badly enough. In the meantime, I have work to attend to."

She exited the room, leaving Jacen and me alone.

"What are you staring at?" he growled at me. "Don't you have work to do, too? A kingdom to help Laila run?"

"Of course." I nodded. "But I also wanted to let you know that I'm here for you, if you ever want to talk."

"Don't play that game with me." He scowled.

"What game?" I reached for the amulet again, forming my expression into one that I hoped looked like complete innocence.

"The game where you pretend to care about anyone except for yourself."

"There's no pretense here," I told him. "I *do* care about you. I want you to become the strongest vampire prince that ever lived. Perhaps even a king."

"I'll never become a king." He crossed his arms. "I don't *want* to become a king."

"Then what do you want?" I asked, truly curious.

"To be human again."

"Why?" I laughed. "Even if that were possible—which it isn't—why would you refuse the power you've been given? Why would you want to be so weak?"

"I'm not going to bother explaining it to you," he looked away from me and walked over to the window, gazing longingly at the human village below. "You'll never understand."

"I might understand more than you think." I slithered toward him, and when I was close enough, I laid my hand gently on his shoulder. "I understand that you need comfort, Jacen. I can provide that. Let me give it to you."

I leaned forward, looking deep into his eyes, my lips

getting closer and closer to his. What would kissing him feel like? I imagined that old man's blood must still coat his tongue—I wished I could know how delicious it tasted to him.

It must have been incredible, to make him lose control like he did.

"Stop." He stepped back, his eyes dilating as he stared into mine. "Leave my quarters. Now."

"Are you trying to compel me?" I laughed again, although disappointment fluttered in my stomach. I wouldn't be turned away that easily. Instead, I leaned forward again, willing him to give into temptation. He'd given in with that human. Why not with me?

He simply backed away and repeated his command.

"You know I'm wearing wormwood," I continued, reaching for my necklace. "Your compulsion won't work on me."

Compulsion was an ability that only the originals—and the vampires they directly turned—possessed. It was the ability to make others do as they willed. It could be used to achieve greatness, but it could also be used to achieve great destruction. Which was why the originals were extremely selective in who they turned into a vampire prince or princess.

They couldn't risk creating a vampire who might use the powers they'd been gifted to destroy their own sire.

"We're done here." He took another step away from me, narrowing his eyes. "Unless you have anything more you need to say?"

"No," I said. "At least, not now."

With that, I turned on my heel and headed out the door. Fire ran through my veins as I stomped down the hall—frustration. I hated not getting what I wanted.

Jacen may not want me now. But in time, he would learn to.

Because eventually, I would be his queen.

5: ANNIKA

I HELD OUT MY ARM, watching as the needle sucked the blood from the crease of my elbow and into the clear vial. I sat there for ten minutes, staring blankly ahead as I did my monthly duty as a citizen of the Vale.

Like all humans who lived in the kingdom, I was required to donate blood once a month.

This was my twelfth time donating blood.

Twelve months. One year. That's how long it had been since my family had been murdered in front of my eyes and I'd been kidnapped to the Vale.

When I'd first been told that I was now a blood slave to vampires, I didn't believe it. Vampires were supposed to be *fiction*. They didn't exist in real life.

But I couldn't deny what I'd seen in front of my eyes. Those pale men, how quickly they'd moved, how they'd ripped their teeth into my parents and brother's throats and drained them dry, leaving their corpses at the bottom of that ski trail.

Why had I been the one chosen to live, and not them?

It was all because I'd fallen on that slope. If I hadn't fallen, I would have been first down the mountain. I would have been killed. My mom would have been last, and *she* would have been the one taken.

But my mom wouldn't have been strong enough to survive in the Vale. So even though I hated that I'd lived while they'd died, it was better that I lived in this hellish prison than any of them. I'd always been strong. Stubborn. Determined.

Those traits kept me going every day. They were the traits that kept me *alive*.

At first, I'd wanted to escape. I thought that if I could just get out of this cursed village, I could run to the nearest town and get help. I could save all the humans who were trapped in the Vale.

I didn't get far before a wolf tried to attack me.

I'd used my gymnastics skills to climb high up on a tree, but if Mike hadn't followed me, fought off the wolf, and dragged me back inside the Vale, I would have been dead meat. The wolves would have eventually gotten to me and feasted upon my body, leaving nothing but bones.

Mike had told me everything about the wolves as we'd walked back to the Tavern. He'd grown up in the Vale, so he knew a lot about its history. He'd told me that they weren't regular wolves—they were shifters. They'd made a pact with the vampires centuries ago, after the vampires had invaded their land and claimed this valley as their own. He'd told me about how the wolves craved human flesh as much as the vampires craved human blood, and how if a human tried to escape—if they crossed the line of the Vale—they became dinner to the wolves.

At least the vampires let us live, so they could have a continuous supply of blood to feast upon whenever they wanted.

The wolves just killed on the spot.

That was the first and last time I'd tried to escape. And after Mike had saved me, we'd become best friends. He'd offered me my job at the Tavern, where I'd been working—and living—ever since. All of us who worked there lived in the small rooms above the bar, sleeping in the bunks inside.

He and the others had helped me cope with the transition—with realizing I was a slave to the vampires, and that as a mere human amongst supernaturals, there was no way out.

They were my family now.

"You're done," the nurse said, removing the needle from my arm. She placed a Band-Aid on the bleeding dot, and I flexed my elbow, trying to get some feeling back in the area. "See you next month."

"Yeah." I gathered my bag and stood up. "Bye."

On my way out, I passed Martha—the youngest girl who worked at the Tavern. She slept in the bunk above mine, and along with being the youngest, she was also the smallest.

It took her twice as long to recover from the blood loss as it did for me.

"Good luck," I told her on the way out. "I'll see you back at the Tavern." I winked, and she smiled, since she knew what I was about to do.

It was what I always did on blood donation day.

I held my bag tightly to my side and stepped onto the street, taking a deep breath of the cold mountain air. It was dark—us humans were forced to adjust to the vampires' nocturnal schedule—and I could see my breath in front of me. The witch who'd created the shield to keep the Vale hidden from human eyes also regulated the temperature, but she could only do so much. And since it was December in Canada, it was naturally still cold.

I hurried to the busiest street in town—Main Street, as it was so creatively named. Humans manned stalls, and vampires walked around, purchasing luxuries that only they were afforded. Meat, doughnuts, pizza, cheeses—you name it, the vampires bought it.

The vampires didn't even *need* food to survive, but they ate it anyway, because it tasted good.

Us humans, on the other hand, were relegated to porridge, bread, rice, and beans—the bare necessities. The vampires thought of us as nothing but cattle—as blood banks. And blood banks didn't deserve food for enjoyment. Only for nourishment.

Luckily, Mike had taught me a trick or two since the day he'd saved me from the wolves. After seeing me climb that tree, he'd called me "scrappy" and said it was a skill that would get me far in the Vale.

He'd taught me how to steal.

It was ironic, really. Stealing hadn't been something that had ever crossed my mind in my former life. I used to have it good—successful, loving parents, trips to the Caribbean in the spring, skiing out west in the winter, and an occasional voyage to Europe thrown in during the summers. I'd had a credit card, and when I'd needed something, I would buy it without a second thought.

I hadn't appreciated how good I'd had it until all of that was snatched away and I was left with nothing.

Now I walked past the various booths, eyeing up the delicious food I wasn't allowed to have. But more than the food, I was eying up the shopkeepers and the vampires around them. Who seemed most oblivious? Or absorbed in conversation?

It didn't take long to spot a vampire woman flirting with a handsome human shopkeeper. I'd seen enough of vampires as a species to know that if the flirting was going to progress anywhere, it would lead to him becoming one of her personal blood slaves, but he followed her every movement, entranced by her attention.

They were the only two people at the booth. Everyone else was going about their own business, not paying any attention to me—the small, orphaned blood slave with downcast eyes and torn up jeans.

Which gave me the perfect opportunity to snatch the food that us humans were forbidden to purchase.

Sparks will fly once Jacen and Annika meet, so go to mybook.to/vampirewishpaperback to grab The Vampire Wish on Amazon and continue reading!

ABOUT THE AUTHOR

Michelle Madow is a USA Today bestselling author of fast paced fantasy novels that will leave you turning the pages wanting more! Go to michellemadow.com/books to view a full list of Michelle's novels.

She grew up in Maryland and now lives in Florida. Some of her favorite things are: reading, traveling, pizza, time travel, Broadway musicals, and spending time with friends and family. Someday, she hopes to travel the world for a year on a cruise ship.

To get free books, exclusive content, and instant updates from Michelle, visit www.michellemadow.com/subscribe and subscribe to her newsletter now!

www.michellemadow.com
michelle@madow.com

THE VAMPIRE RULES

Published by Dreamscape Publishing

Copyright © 2018 Michelle Madow

ISBN-10: 1983549207
ISBN-13: 978-1983549205

❀ Created with Vellum

Manufactured by Amazon.ca
Bolton, ON